HODDER CHILDREN'S BOOKS

First published in Great Britain in 2015 by Hodder and Stoughton

6

A CIP catalogue record for this book
is available from the British Library.

ISBN 978 1 444 92227 1

Printed and bound in Great Britain
by Clays Ltd, St Ives plc

The paper and board used in this book
are made from wood from responsible sources

Hodder Children's Books
An imprint of
Hachette Children's Group
Part of Hodder and Stoughton
Carmelite House
50 Victoria Embankment
London EC4Y 0DZ

An Hachette UK Company
www.hachette.co.uk

www.hachettechildrens.co.uk

For the one and only Mr Melling, with love
VF

To Leo-Branko Sunajko
DM

Godfrey

Sam J. Butterbiggins
and Dandy the doodlebird

The Well

Prunella

Uncle Archibald

Aunt Eglantine

A BOTHERSOME BREAKFAST

Dear diary,

My number one ambition is to change
my name.

This is because my number two (and
most important) ambition is to be
a Very Noble Knight, and Very Noble
Knights are not called Sam.

Sam sighed, and looked at the doodlebird beside him. "It's not fair, Dandy. Mother's called Oleander-Breeze, and Father's called Fitzwulliam-Wulliam. Wouldn't you think they could have come up with something better than Sam? Lord Sam Butterbiggins doesn't sound in the least bit noble."

The doodlebird looked sympathetic.

"What do you think about Gilderoso the Magnificent?" Sam asked.

The doodlebird scratched his head, but didn't seem to have much of an opinion. Sam sucked the end of his pen, and went on with his list.

Number three ambition: I want to be a Very Noble Knight with silver armour and a snow white steed. (That's the kind of horse Very Noble Knights have.)

Number four ambition: I want to go on quests. If I change my name I'm sure I

Tingalinga bang bang bang!!!!!

Sam dropped his pen at the sound of the breakfast bell and jumped off the bed. Aunt Eglantine was very fussy about people being on time for meals. On his first day at Mothscale Castle Sam had tried to explain that because his room was in the topmost turret he had further to come than everyone else, but Aunt Egg had taken no notice.

"Bad manners, Samuel, are only for pigs."

Sam had made the mistake of asking, "What about sheep?" and Aunt Egg had peered at him. "Samuel, I hope you aren't going to be a DIFFICULT child. When I told your dear mama that you could stay here, I did not expect a DIFFICULT boy."

"Sorry, Aunt Egg." Sam had not meant to be difficult, and from then on he tried his best to get to meals on time.

PLAN for getting to meals on time.

1. Slide down the bannisters? X
No bannisters. There might have been once, but now there's only a piece of rope.
Don't want blisters.

2. Parachute out of window? X
No parachute. And Aunt Egg v fussy about
sheets. Doodlebird says NOT to use umbrella.

3. Take stairs six at a time? X
Not six. Doodlebird thinks bad idea
to show Aunt Egg torn trousers.

4. Take stairs three at a time?
YES! RESULT!

Now he had been at Mothscale Castle for a week Sam was much better at jumping down the two hundred and fifty-two steps, but today he stopped halfway. He had been thinking of knightly names, and a particularly brilliant idea had struck him.

"YES!" he said, and punched the air. Then, remembering where he was, he hurried on down to the breakfast room and took his seat. His uncle Archibald was reading the *Palace Times*, and his cousin Prune was eating cereal

and milk in a splashy kind of way.

Aunt Eglantine was trying to teach a very small dragon to sit at the table, without much success.

"Good morning, Aunt Egg," Sam said. His aunt liked him to be polite. "I was thinking I might change my name. Could you please call me Gilderoso the Magnificent from now on?"

Aunt Egg didn't even look up. "Nonsense, Sam. You've got a perfectly good name. And you're late. Now eat your cereal. There's no porridge today. Godfrey! NO!" And Aunt Egg picked the little dragon off the table, where he was trying to lick the marmalade off of Uncle Archibald's plate.

"Vulcan the Indestructible?" Sam said hopefully.

Prune burst into giggles. "VULCAN? What sort of name is THAT?"

Sam reached for the milk.

"That's a bit unfair," he said, "considering you're called Prune."

"It's short for Prunella, stupid," Prune said crossly, and she threw a bread roll at Sam. The bread roll missed, and hit Godfrey instead.

Godfrey let out a wail and fell off his chair.

Aunt Egg looked furious. "Really, children! Queen Josephine is expecting me to return this dragon in the peak of condition! Whatever will she say if he goes home a nervous wreck?"

"Sorry, Aunt Eglantine," Sam muttered.

Prune made a face. "I don't see why we have to have stupid dragons to stay anyway."

There was a protesting squeak from under the table.

Aunt Egg rose to her feet, her face very red. "Princess Prunella! You know very well – at least, you would if you listened – that your father and I are suffering from Severe Lack of Funds!"

Prune looked mystified.

Sam gave a small cough. "No cash!" he whispered.

Aunt Eglantine glared at him. "If we didn't offer Luxury Holiday Accommodation for

12

Dragons, Griffins and Other
Regal Beasts, Prunella, you
would NOT be living the comfortable life
you do."

Prune sniggered. "What about dear little
Sam the spam? What's he doing here? Is he a
regal beast as well?"

Aunt Egg tried her crushing stare on Prune,
but to no effect. Prune remained uncrushed.

"Sam's parents have gone away on a very
important promotional tour. If your father
and I were to do the same, you'd be sent to
stay with Aunt Oleander-Breeze and Uncle
Fitzwulliam-Wulliam. Now, I'm off to polish
the griffins. Lady Stickle is collecting them
later today, and I want them looking their
best. Prunella, I expect you to keep an eye
on Godfrey. And whatever you do, don't let
him out!"

As her mother sailed out of the breakfast room, Prune waved her spoon in the air. "I'd never go and stay with you, Sam Butterbiggins." She rolled her eyes in mock horror. "Never! You live in a potty little castle. It doesn't even have a drawbridge."

"Yes it does!" Sam said indignantly.

"It so does not." Prune folded her arms.

Sam stood up, tripped over Godfrey, and stomped the two hundred and fifty-two steps back to his room. He crashed inside and slammed the door behind him.

WHERE'S GODFREY?

It's cold and wet and all I can see from my window is miles and miles and miles of creepy forest.

Sometimes I hear howling. I'm sure it's wolves.

I hate it here.

Prune is the most horrible cousin in the whole wide world.

Must remember: write postcard to Mother and Father INSISTING they take me away. Will tell them I have spots. Might be true. Prune is horrible enough to give anyone spots.

"I DON'T live in a potty little castle," he growled as he wrote. "It's MUCH nicer than this horrible old dump!"

The doodlebird sneezed, spattering ink all over Sam's diary.

"AWK!" He flapped a wing, and looked apologetic. "AWK AWK AWK!"

Sam pulled out a grubby hanky and dabbed at the splatters. The result was not a success.

"Oops." Sam peered doubtfully at the blots and smears. "Ma won't be pleased. She went on and on and ON about keeping my diary tidy." He sighed. "She said she wants to know every single thing I do while she and Pa are away." A thought came to him, and he looked at the doodlebird. "Do you think that means I should tell her Prune called our castle potty?"

"AW AW AWK?" The doodlebird put his head

on one side, and Sam grinned.

"Well – maybe I shouldn't tell her
EVERYTHING."

He looked up at the portrait on the wall
above his bed. His parents, Lord Fitzwulliam
and Lady Oleander Butterbiggins, leered back.

The artist was a friend of Lady Oleander's,
and usually painted pictures of vegetables, but
she had done her best. Sam, studying the two

potatoes wearing lopsided coronets, wondered if his parents had thought to pack a picture of him. He suspected they hadn't.

He sighed again. "All I want is to go on a quest, Dandy. I want to go on loads of quests, actually, and if I win enough of them I'll be made a knight. And that's what I want more than anything in the whole wide world."

BANG BANG BANG THUMP!!

Dandy flew up in a flurry of feathers, knocking the ink bottle over. Sam rushed to open the door. On the other side was Prune, and Sam's eyes opened wide as he stared at her. She was covered in mud, and scowling horribly.

"What—" he began.

Prune stamped her foot. Water squelched

out from her shoe, and the doodlebird flew up to the top of the wardrobe in alarm.

"It's all YOUR fault!" she said. "It's YOUR fault, and you've got to sort it out!"

Sam glared at her. "I'm not sorting anything out for you, Princess Prune! You said my castle was potty!"

Prune squelched her way across the room and flumped down on Sam's bed. "Well, it is. But I'll say it isn't just as long as you help me get Godfrey out of the well."

"Godfrey?" Sam said blankly. "Who's Godfrey?"

Prune picked up Sam's pillow and threw it at him. "Don't be so STUPID! Godfrey's that dragon you tripped over when you went off in a huff. You tripped over him, and I laughed, and he went TOTALLY mad and flew out of the window! And we didn't even know he could fly! And Pa actually stopped reading his paper. He said, 'I say, Prunella old thing! That won't do. Won't do at all! Fetch that beast back right this minute, before your mother gets back. Jump to it!'"

Prune's imitation of Uncle Archibald was so good that Sam couldn't help smiling.

"But what's Godfrey doing in a well?" he asked.

For the first time, Prune looked awkward. "Um. I tried to catch him, but he kept flapping away just out of reach, so I had to run faster and faster – and then I slipped over. And Godfrey stood and squawked EXACTLY as if he thought me being covered in mud was the funniest thing ever, so I shouted at him and he zoomed away – and he wasn't looking where he was going and he fell down the well in Ma's garden!" She jumped off the bed. "And we need to get him out! Come ON!"

"Just a minute …" Sam scratched his head. "Why can't he fly out of the well?"

The doodlebird coughed. "AWK! AWK AWK AWK AWK!"

Prune looked up. "What's THAT?"

"That's Dandy.

He's my doodlebird."

Sam gave Dandy a little wave. "He says dragons can't fly straight upwards."

Prune snorted. "Oh yes? How does HE know?"

"He knows lots of things." Sam frowned. "More than you, anyway."

"If he's so clever," Prune snapped, "ask him how we get Godfrey out!"

"AWK AWK". The doodlebird shook his head. "AWK!"

Sam looked at his cousin. "He says you have to say you're sorry you called our castle potty, and then he'll—"

"AWK!" The doodlebird sounded most indignant, and Prune gave a sudden giggle.

"No he didn't!"

Reluctantly, Sam grinned back at her.

"No. He said it might be difficult."

"Then you've GOT to come and help me! If we don't get him out Pa'll get really REALLY furious. He said …" Prune gulped. "He said he'd take Weebles away if I didn't get Godfrey back before Ma finds out he's missing – and I couldn't BEAR it if I didn't have Weebles!"

"Who's Weebles?" Sam asked.

Prune grabbed his arm, and began to haul him towards the door.

"My pony. Oh, DO come on! I'll … I'll even call you Gilderwotsit if you will!"

An amazing thought zoomed into Sam's head. Rescuing Godfrey would be a Noble Deed! And doing Noble Deeds was what knights did!

Maybe this was his very first quest?

"OK," he said.

A BRILLIANT IDEA!

As Sam leapt down the stairs behind Prune, he was feeling happier than he had all morning. He imagined a cheery Uncle Archibald clapping him on the back, saying, "Well done, young man. You are definitely worthy of being a knight! Let me present you with—"

Sam's daydream was interrupted by the real Uncle Archibald. He was standing at the bottom of the stairs, and he did NOT look cheery.

"Prunella? Have you found that dragon yet, what what what? Your mother won't be out much longer, and I've warned you – no dragon, no Weebles! It's been a bad enough morning as it is. Cook couldn't get the oven to light, so no toast," Uncle Archibald shook his head sadly, "and no porridge, and you know how much your mother loves her porridge. Can't have her upset again."

"It's all OK, Pa," Prune told him, and Sam looked at her in surprise. "I've got Godfrey trapped, so he can't escape. Sam's coming to help find him something to eat."

"Good show! Glad to hear it." Uncle Archibald gave

a brisk nod, and sailed off into his office, the newspaper under his arm.

Sam pulled at Prune's sleeve. "Why did you tell him we'd got Godfrey trapped?"

Prune gave him a sour look. "Well – he is, isn't he? He can't get out of the well. Your doodlebird said so. Don't be silly."

Sam didn't answer. He followed Prune out of the castle, muttering to himself, "She's HORRIBLE! If I wasn't trying to be a Very Noble Knight I'd … I'd go back to bed."

Outside the castle was a courtyard, and beyond the courtyard was an archway and a path leading to Aunt Egg's flower and vegetable garden. As Sam trailed behind Prune, he could see why she had fallen over. It had been raining all night, and Sam's shoes were heavy with mud by the time they reached the well.

Aunt Egg had arranged pots of geraniums and larkspur round the edge, together with several merry gnomes. She liked to think the result was an Artistic Feature, and it was mentioned in all her brochures. She would not have been happy if she had seen her daughter pulling two of the pots to one side and pushing a gnome out of the way.

"Godfrey's down there," Prune announced.

"All you have to do is go and get him."

Sam didn't move, and Prune gave him a shove. "Go on!"

Sam took a deep breath. "No. Well, not unless you start being a bit nicer. You think I'm silly, but I'll tell YOU something! You're rude, and you're horrible."

There was a long silence, while Prune stared at him.

"So?" Sam folded his arms. "Are you going to say you're sorry?"

Two large tears trickled down Prune's face, and she gave a loud hiccup. "Ma's always busy with her stupid animals and Pa's always reading his paper and Weebles is the only one who cares about me … I CAN'T lose Weebles!"

"Then try to be nice." Sam sighed, and went to peer into the well. It was dark, and at first he couldn't see anything, but gradually he began to make out bunches of weed and murky water at the bottom. There was no sign of Godfrey, but as Sam stared down he heard a small sneeze. Leaning further over he saw the little dragon had found a hole where several bricks were missing, and was crouched inside with his tail sticking out.

"I can see him!"

Prune came to stand beside Sam. "Can we climb down?"

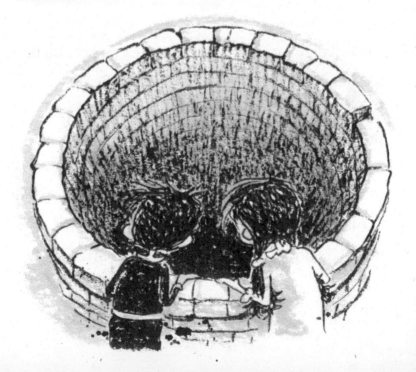

Sam looked at the green slimy walls, but there was no sign of any kind of ladder. "We need a rope. Doesn't Aunt Egg use the well to water her flowers? I thought all wells had buckets and ropes."

"I think she makes Higgins do the watering," Prune said. She shook her head. "And we can't ask him. He'll tell Ma for sure."

Sam squinted into the darkness. "Godfrey!" he called. "Can you hear me?"

There was a scrabbling noise, and Godfrey's head appeared. He peered up at Sam, and gave a mournful squeak.

"It's OK," Sam told him. "We're here to rescue you!"

Godfrey squeaked again and edged further forward ... and a large chunk of brick crumbled and fell into the water with a loud PLOP! The little dragon gave an alarmed

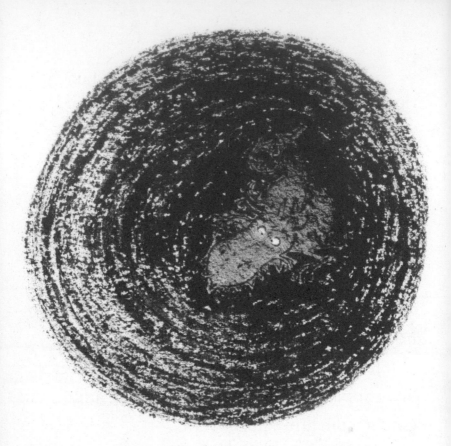

"Eeeek!" and wriggled back into his hiding place.

Prune gave a gasp of horror. "He's not safe!"

"He's got to keep still," Sam said. "Dandy – can dragons swim?"

Dandy looked doubtful. "AKK AKK AWK."

"He doesn't think they can," Sam translated.

The doodlebird hopped onto the edge of
the well, and called down,

"AWK AWK?"

Even Prune knew what the
answering squeak meant.
"Dragons can't swim."

The squeak was
followed by a series of
sneezes, and Prune gave a loud wail. "He's
catching a cold! That's all we need ... Come
on, Sam! Think of something!" She rubbed her
eyes, leaving muddy smears all over her face.
"We've got to get him out! Oh, PLEASE, Sam!"

Sam felt a sudden glow. Prune had said
please. She really, REALLY needed him.
And he, Sam J. Butterbiggins, was going to
help her!

He squared his shoulders and smiled at
Prune. "Don't worry. I'll—"

"AWK!!!!"

The doodlebird landed on Sam's shoulder.

"AK AK AWK!"

"WOW!" Sam
beamed. "GENIUS
idea! Wait here,
Prune. Don't let
Godfrey move. Sing
to him or something!
I'll be back in two ticks!"
And he dashed off as fast as
he could go, leaving Prune staring after him.

"AWK," said the doodlebird, and bobbed his
head at her. "AWK?"

"I don't know what you mean," Prune told
him. "But if you're asking if I'm all right,
no I'm not."

Sam rushed out of the garden, across the courtyard, over the drawbridge and into the castle. Pounding across the hall he headed for the stairs, and leapt up three steps at a time until he reached the landing that led to the tower and his bedroom.

"YES!" He grabbed at the rope that made do for a bannister. It was tied to a huge iron

ring, but Sam had no time to untangle knots.

He gave the rope a sharp tug, and it came away from the wall in a shower of dust and spiders. Looping it over his shoulder, he hurried round and round the spiral staircase to the top, where he tried to pull the other end free. This wasn't so easy – however hard Sam tugged, the iron ring held firm. He tried to undo the knot, but it was impossible. Years of use had turned the strands of rope into a solid greasy lump.

"Rats!" Sam said, and he dashed into his room and leant out of the window. "Dandy!" he yelled, "I need you!"

There was a flurry of wings, and the doodlebird landed beside him.

"Awk?"

"Can you undo that knot?" Sam asked. "Or think of a way of cutting the rope free? I can't get it away from the wall!"

The doodlebird hopped across the room and peered closely at the knot. Then, with half a dozen stabs of his beak, he reduced it to a few wisps of string.

"YES! Thanks, Dandy!"

Sam snatched up the rope with a whoop of triumph and headed for the stairs. Taking them three at a time again, he hurtled downwards, arriving at the bottom with a crash. Picking himself up, he shot towards the front door, only to be stopped by the substantial stomach of Uncle Archibald.

"Steady on there, old chap! What's the hurry?" His uncle bent down, and inspected Sam. "Egg's nephew, isn't it? What's your name again?"

Sam blinked. "Erm … Sam, sir. Sam Butterbiggins."

"Butterbiggins, eh?" Uncle Archibald looked disapproving. "Any relation to that dreadful old trout Oleander-Breeze?'

"Um … yes," Sam said. "Actually, she's my mother."

"Oh well. Can't be helped." Uncle Archibald gave Sam a consoling pat. "Enjoying it here, are you? Playing a game, what what what?"

Sam hid the rope behind his back, and did his best to smile happily. "Yes, Uncle Archibald. I'm having a great time. We're playing …" He swallowed. What could he say? Inspiration came to him. "Hide and Seek!"

"Hide and Seek, eh?" His uncle raised his eyebrows. "In my day we used to practise being knights. Bit of jousting here, bit of dragon spotting there. Suppose you young fellas don't care for that kind of thing, though."

Sam gazed at Uncle Archibald, his eyes shining. "Oh, but I DO! Uncle Archibald, do you think I could ever be a real knight?"

"What's that?" Uncle Archibald put his hand to his ear as if he couldn't believe what he'd heard. "You want to be a knight?"

"More than anything in the world," Sam said. "But I don't know what I have to do. Can you tell me?"

Uncle Archibald stroked his chin. "You'll need to follow the rules, young fellow. Same as we did. Follow the rules – that's the ticket!"

"Rules? What rules? Where can I find them? Where are they? Please, PLEASE tell me!" Sam pleaded.

"Harrumph." The old man heaved a sigh.

"Now there's a problem. Lost. Gone. Don't know where. But I can tell you rule one, if you like."

"Oh YES!" Sam said. "I'd like that VERY MUCH INDEED!"

"Find yourself a True Companion." Uncle Archibald beamed at his nephew. "There you go. That's rule one."

"A True Companion," Sam repeated. "I'll do that." He hesitated, then asked, "I don't suppose you remember the next one as well?"

His uncle didn't answer. He was looking into the distance, a happy smile on his whiskery face. "Used to play with my brother. Of course, when we grew up we found armour was dreadfully uncomfortable. Beastly heavy stuff, armour. And the goblins and the giants were always a tricky lot.

Didn't play fair. By Jove! I remember ..."

His voice died away. Sam, breathless with excitement, whispered, "Yes?"

Uncle Archibald snapped back into the present. "No, no. You don't want to hear about the good old ... the old times." He looked guiltily over his shoulder. "Egg doesn't like me talking about them. Says we should live in the present. Quite right too! Always right, your aunt Eglantine. Splendid woman! Off you go, young ... What was your name again?"

"Sam." Sam winced as his uncle gave him a hearty slap on the back.

"Of course! Off you go, young Sam, and play. Prune caught that dragon yet?"

Taken aback by the sudden question, Sam jumped. "No – I mean, yes! We found him in the garden."

Which was true, Sam told himself.

Absolutely true, even if they hadn't quite caught Godfrey.

"Good stuff. Carry on! As you were!" And Uncle Archibald marched away.

Sam took a deep breath, and headed for the well. "I'm going to be a knight," he told himself. "If I can only find the rules ... and I'll need a True Companion! Would the doodlebird be OK? He's my best friend. But do birds count?"

Sam heard Prune before he saw her – she was singing "Twinkle, Twinkle, Little Star" in a tuneless drone. When Sam arrived she put her finger to her lips.

"Godfrey's asleep," she whispered. "He kept wriggling about and knocking bits of brick into the water, so I sang him to sleep."

"That was clever," Sam said.

Prune looked smug. "I am." She gave Sam a sharp look. "You look very pleased with yourself. What have you been doing?"

Sam dithered. Should he tell Prune about his conversation with Uncle Archibald? But that would mean telling her he wanted to be a knight, and she was bound to laugh at him. "Um ... I've got the rope!"

"You're up to something," Prune said, but she didn't ask any more questions.

Sam, relieved, unravelled the rope, and looked round for something to tie it to. A nearby tree seemed to be the obvious answer, and he took time making sure his knot was a strong one. Then, metre by metre, he carefully lowered the other end into the well, doing his best not to make a splash.

"I think it's safe," he said as he gave the rope a tug. "Do you want to go and get him? He knows you better than me."

Before Prune could say anything, the doodlebird lifted a warning wing. "AK AK AWK!"

"Oh." Sam's face creased into a puzzled frown. "You're right."

He turned to Prune. "How are we going to hold onto Godfrey and climb back up the rope?"

"If we had a bag, you could hang it round your neck," Prune suggested. "Hang on. I'll go and look in Higgins's tool shed." And she was gone, leaving Sam standing holding the rope.

"Huh," he said to the doodlebird. "Did you notice? She said, 'YOU could hang it round YOUR neck'. She's obviously not going down the well herself."

Dandy put his head on one side. "Awk Awk Ak Ak Ak," he remarked.

"Really? Godfrey doesn't like her? Why not?" Sam asked.

"Ak," explained the doodlebird. "Ak Awk."

Sam smiled.

"Because she laughed at him? I don't like it when she laughs at me, either. But do you know what, Dandy? She's not as bad as I thought she was."

"Who's not as bad as you thought they were?" Prune had come silently over the muddy grass, and was staring at him suspiciously. "I hope you don't mean me!"

"Erm ... of course not," Sam lied.

Prune decided to give her cousin the benefit of the doubt. "I suppose I'll have to believe you. Here's the bag. I chose the one with the longest handles." And she handed Sam a large green bag smelling strongly of onions.

"Yuck!" Sam wrinkled his nose. "Do you think Godfrey will get in that?"

"Why not?" Prune asked. "He wants to be rescued, doesn't he?"

"Yes ... but he's not exactly clever, is he?"

Sam sniffed again at the bag. "The smell might put him off."

"Only one way to find out," Prune said firmly.

Before the discussion could go any further, the doodlebird, who was perched on the edge of the well, gave a loud squawk.

"AWK!" he said in alarm. "AWK AWK AWK!"

Sam and Prune rushed to see what he was looking at, and saw that Godfrey was balanced precariously on the very edge of the broken bricks. He was hissing angrily, and tiny puffs of smoke were coming out of his nostrils as he glared up at the worried faces above him.

"QUICK," said Sam.
"Give me that bag!" And he
began to climb down the
rope.

It was not an easy climb.
The bag round his neck got
in Sam's way, and the walls of
the well were slimy with green
weed. Gritting his teeth, he
made his way down as fast as
he could until he was level
with the little dragon.

"Good boy, Godfrey!"
he said. "I've come to
rescue you!"

Godfrey hissed, and blew
smoke rings in his rescuer's eyes.

"Ooof!" Sam coughed. "Don't
you want to be rescued?"

Godfrey hissed again. A chunk of brick broke underneath him, and he gave a squeak of terror and backed away. As the dragon retreated, Sam saw that what he and Prune had thought was a gap in the bricks was, in fact, the entrance to a hole. It was quite deep, and the curved bricks round the entrance suggested it had been made for a purpose.

"Could it be a secret hiding place?" Sam wondered out loud. And then, "However am I going to get Godfrey out? He's right at the back now, and I don't think my arm is long enough to reach him."

"Have you caught him yet?" Prune called down.

Sam began to shake his head, but realising he couldn't be seen in the darkness, called back, "No! I don't think he wants to be rescued!"

"What?" Prune sounded as if she didn't believe him. "Of course he does!"

Sam peered at Godfrey. Godfrey shut his eyes.

"PLEASE, Godfrey!" Sam begged. "Be a good dragon! Do come out!"

There was no response and Sam, clinging to the rope with one hand, stretched the other towards the dragon. His fingers touched not scales, but something flat and papery.

"Funny place to hide something," he thought. "Must have been there for AGES!" and he carefully pulled it towards him and dropped it into the bag hanging round his neck.

There was an agonised whisper from above him. "Sam! I've just seen Ma! She's got the griffins on a lead, and she's coming this way!"

Sam, whose arms were aching badly, climbed back up the rope and rolled over the well's edge.

"Oh no! Don't let her see Godfrey!" he said. "Pretend we're playing a game! I told Uncle Archibald we were playing Hide and Seek!"

Prune wasn't listening. She was staring at her mother as she began to march towards the the vegetable garden, willing her to change direction. Two or three steps in, Aunt Egg stopped, and both Sam and Prune held their breath as she began to inspect the mud on the griffins' paws with an expression of deep disapproval.

"Galumphing cuttlefish!" she said.
"We can't have this! Mud on your
paws, lads? That'll NEVER do!
Come on. We'll go round the back,
and I'll give you one final polish
before Mummy comes to collect
her little sweethearts." And with
an encouraging whistle she led
the two griffins towards
the courtyard.

"PHEW!" Sam sank back against the well, and Prune heaved a sigh of relief.

"That was SCARY! But we'll have to hurry. She'll be asking about Godfrey any minute now."

Sam was rubbing his arms. "I don't think I can go down that rope again. My arms feel as if they're about twenty metres long. You'll have to try."

Prune went pale, and for a moment Sam thought she was going to cry. "Can't your doodlebird go?"

"AWK!" The doodlebird's feathers stood straight up on end. "AWK!"

Prune shook her head. "I suppose not. But …" She swallowed hard. "I can't go down. I … I can't swim."

Sam leant towards her and patted her hand. "I only learnt to swim last year."

Prune snatched her hand away.

"Well, don't think that makes you better than me," she said, but she didn't sound as sharp as she usually did. "So what'll we do now?"

"Maybe we could let the bag down on the end of the rope?" Sam suggested.

"But how would we make Godfrey get inside?" Prune wanted to know. "He doesn't seem to like either of us much."

"No." Sam rubbed at his ear. "I was thinking about that." He lowered his voice. "I don't think I ought to have said that he's not very clever."

He waited for Prune to tell him that it was all his fault, but she didn't. Instead she said, "Maybe I shouldn't have laughed at him."

The doodlebird put his head on one side.
"A͞K A͞K A͞WK. A͞K A͞K A͞WK?"

Sam slapped his head, and leapt to his feet.
"OF COURSE!" He turned to Prune. "Did you hear what he said? MARMALADE!"

Prune looked blank. "Marmalade?"

"Don't you remember? Godfrey kept trying to lick the marmalade off of Uncle Archibald's

plate at breakfast! Where can we find some?"
Sam was dancing up and down in excitement.

"The kitchen!"

And Prune was gone.

While he was waiting for Prune to come back,
Sam hauled the dripping rope out of the well,
and – with some difficulty – managed to tie
the gardener's bag to the end. As he did so
he remembered the flat, papery thing he had
found, and pulled it out. It was a battered-
looking parchment scroll that had seen better
days – Godfrey had flattened it and covered
it in muddy footprints, and as Sam tried to
unfold it, a grumpy spider scuttled out.

The doodlebird gave a squawk
of joy and swooped down.
"AK," he remarked as he
finished his unexpected
snack. "AK."

Sam took no notice. He was staring, wide-eyed, at the crabbed and crooked writing.

Greetings to all who wish to be Truly Noble Knights. Herewith we offer you the tasks that should be accomplished, in order as hereby listed, that ye may succeed.

Sam put the scroll down, his heart beating wildly. "It's the rules! The rules Uncle Archibald was talking about! And I've found them! I've actually FOUND THEM!"

"Sam! Sam!" It was Prune calling him, and he hastily tucked the scroll into his pocket as his cousin arrived in a rush, clutching a jar of marmalade and purple in the face.

"It was AWFUL!" she gasped. "I went round the castle so I could sneak into the kitchen through the back door, and when I came out again Ma was standing there talking to those stupid griffins! I had to climb through the pantry window and Cook saw me and she hates me because sometimes I help myself to biscuits and I'm SURE she'll tell Ma – and then I'll be in HUGE trouble and Pa'll take away Weebles and I can't LIVE without my darling Weebles!" She waved the marmalade jar wildly in the air, and Sam sprang forward.

"Careful!" he warned, but it was too late ...

Luckily the jar didn't smash. It landed in the mud, and Sam picked it up and wiped it with his handkerchief.

"Don't worry," he said, with a confidence he didn't entirely feel, "you won't lose your pony. Now, let's see what Godfrey thinks about this ..."

He opened the marmalade and tipped the contents inside the bag. Then, very carefully, he lowered the bag until it was at the level of Godfrey's hideout.

Nothing happened.

"Prune – do you think you could possibly stop sniffing?" Sam asked. "I can't hear if

Godfrey's squeaking or not."

"I'm NOT sniffing," Prune said indignantly.

Sam leant over the well. Prune was right. She wasn't sniffing ... but Godfrey was. A small pointed nose appeared, and as Sam watched the head followed.

"Look!" Sam whispered.

Hardly daring to breathe, Sam and Prune saw Godfrey creep further out, and then – with a leap and twist – he dived into the bag. There were sounds of enthusiastic eating

as Sam hauled on the rope and landed the gardener's green bag and its squirming contents on the grass.

"There you are," Sam said as he handed the bag to Prune. "Come on. Let's get him back inside."

Prune tucked the bag firmly under her arm. "Hurrah! I KNEW I could catch him!"

"I'm sorry?" Sam gave her a stare worthy of Aunt Eglantine herself.

"AWK?" said the doodlebird.

There was a moment of hesitation before Prune said, "OK. WE caught him."

"That's right," said Sam. "WE did."

"AWK," said the doodlebird.

"But it was me that fetched the marmalade," Prune said as they hurried through the arch and back across the courtyard. "And it was me who—"

"Look out!" Sam grabbed her arm. He had seen a carriage rattling up the long tree-lined avenue leading to the castle. "There's someone coming!"

He was only just in time. As the three of them scurried round the corner away from the front door they heard Aunt Egg's booming voice, and the excited yowling of the griffins.

"Who's a clever boy, then? Two clever little boysie woysies! Did you hear your mummy's carriage? She's coming to collect you!"

Aunt Egg's words were almost drowned as the yowling increased in volume, and then there was the sound of a grand carriage coming to a halt.

"Round to the pantry window," Prune ordered, and Sam and the doodlebird did as they were told.

THE VERY
GOOD DEED

The window was still open. Sam climbed through first while Prune held the green bag.

Once he was safely inside, he took charge of Godfrey and Prune scrambled in to join him. The doodlebird came last with a flapping of wings, and Prune shut the window with a bang.

"When should we let Godfrey out?" Sam asked as they crept out of the pantry and into the palace kitchen. "I think he's blowing smoke rings or something – the bag's getting very hot."

"Don't let him out yet," Prune said. "I don't think Mrs Jug likes animals—"

"Princess Prunella! WHAT are you doing in MY kitchen?"

Sam spun round. He hadn't met Aunt Egg's cook before, but the cook in Butterbiggins Castle was a particular friend of his, and he knew that a palace kitchen was a cook's own private kingdom.

"I'm terribly terribly sorry, Mrs Jug," he said quickly. "I know we shouldn't be here – but my cousin was showing me round." He held out his hand. "How do you do? I'm Sam Butterbiggins. This is a very splendid kitchen, by the way."

Mrs Jug was not impressed. "Got the gift of the gab, haven't you, young lad? Well, it may be a splendid kitchen to you, but it's nothing but trouble to me. That there oven went out last night, and nothing I do will make it burn

up again. Wood's damp, and there's no dry
kindling left. It'll be a cold lunch, and a cold
tea, and a cold supper too. And that's that."

Prune was outraged. "Cold supper? Yeuch!"

"Don't you yeuch me, Princess Prunella! Saw you earlier, I did! Up to your old tricks, as usual. Helping yourself to my best homemade  marmalade!" A look of grim satisfaction crossed the cook's face. "Told your ma, I did. Reckon you're in BIG trouble!"

Sam's arms were getting uncomfortably hot, but his mind was working overtime. He elbowed Prune sharply before she could answer, and beamed his best smile. "But we've come to help you, Mrs Jug – haven't we, Prune? I'm sorry about the marmalade, but we needed it for Godfrey!"

"Godfrey?" Mrs Jug put her hands on her hips, and her glare grew fiercer. "And what's a Godfrey, when he's at home?"

"It's a … it's a kind of firelighter."

Sam put the green bag down, and peered inside. A sticky little dragon looked back at him, licking its lips and puffing smoke rings.

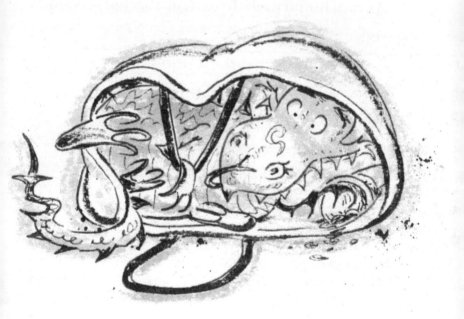

"That's right, Mrs Jug," Prune said. "And he's EVER so good at blowing smoke rings …"

As Prune kept the cook talking, Sam

crouched down to whisper to Godfrey.

"Would you like marmalade every day for breakfast?"

Godfrey considered.

"As much marmalade as you can eat?" Sam offered.

Godfrey put his head on one side. "Eeek?"

"AWK. AK AK AWK AK!" the doodlebird whispered.

Sam stood up. "Mrs Jug … Godfrey says he'll light the oven if he can have some more of your special homemade marmalade."

The cook unbent a little. "Always said my marmalade took a lot of beating. If your Godfrey can light my oven – and I have my doubts about that, seeing as I couldn't get so much as a spark going – he can have all the marmalade he wants."

Sam opened the bag. "Come on, Godfrey!"

With a flick of his tail, the little dragon hopped out of the bag and walked towards the ancient oven. He breathed a couple of smoke rings, and then a blast of flame – and the sticks burst into a cheerful blaze. "Eek," he remarked, and curled himself up on the hearth rug.

"Well I never!" breathed Mrs Jug. "Well I never ever did! That's what I calls a USEFUL animal! Not like them griffins and all. Likely to be staying, is he?"

Before Prune or Sam could explain that Godfrey was only a temporary resident, the kitchen door opened with a crash and Aunt Egg came striding in, followed by Uncle Archibald.

"PRUNELLA!" Aunt Egg roared. "Mrs Jug tells me you've been stealing marmalade! How DARE you, child?"

Sam stood up straight and took a deep breath. "Prune wasn't stealing, Aunt Egg," he began, but he got no further. Mrs Jug put her arm round Prune.

"Seems I was mistaken," she said, "and I begs her pardon. The princess was trying to be helpful, for once in her life." She nodded at Sam. "Her and the lad here – they've got my oven lit. Brought in a little dragon, and as you can see – he's got it going a treat!"

Aunt Egg stared at Prune, and then at Sam. Then she looked at Godfrey, who was licking marmalade off his claws in a contented kind of way.

"Goodness," she said, and sat down at the kitchen table. "Well I never."

Uncle Archibald raised a questioning eyebrow. "Does that mean we'll be having a hot lunch, Mrs Jug?"

"Indeed it does, Your Grace. And – if I might make so bold – I'd like my kitchen clear, so I can get on with what I'm meant to be doing!"

Mrs Jug picked up a saucepan, and Aunt Egg hastily got to her feet.

"Of course," she said. "Prunella! Sam! Take Godfrey, and leave Mrs Jug in peace."

Mrs Jug shook her head. "Leave the little fellow here," she said. "I'll keep an eye on him." She picked up a jar, and ladled a healthy helping of marmalade onto a saucer. "He deserves a treat."

Aunt Egg opened her mouth to object, then thought better of it. "He does seem happy here," she said. "And I don't think he'll ever learn how to sit up at the table like a respectable dragon." She swung back to Prune and Sam. "But WHATEVER have you two been up to? You're covered in mud!"

"They've been playing Knights," Uncle

Archibald told her. "Leave them alone, Egg old bean. Godfrey's been well looked after, and I'd say they've done a good deed. A VERY good deed. Don't know about you, but I'm looking forward to a nice hot lunch!"

And Uncle Archibald took Aunt Egg's arm, and led her towards the door.

As he went, he gave Sam a sly wink, and Sam grinned.

Prune snorted. "What are you grinning at, Sam the spam?"

"Nothing," Sam said.

Mrs Jug raised her saucepan. "Are you leaving, or did I ought to make you?" she enquired.

"We're leaving, Mrs Jug," Sam said, and he and Prune hurried out of the kitchen.

A TRUE
COMPANION

As Sam and Prune walked along the corridor,
Sam put his hand in his pocket to check that
his precious scroll was safe. It rustled, and
without thinking what he was doing he patted
it fondly.

Prune stopped dead. "What have you got
there?" she asked. "And what did Pa mean
when he said we'd been playing Knights?"

Sam, much to his
annoyance, found he
was blushing. "Nothing,"
he said.

"That's rubbish."
Prune gave him a hard
stare. "Pa winked at you.

I saw him. What are you up to?" She came closer. "Is it a game?"

"No." Sam shook his head. "It isn't."

"Ha! I KNEW you were up to something!" Prune was triumphant. "If I promise not to call you Sam the spam, will you tell me?"

Sam looked at his cousin thoughtfully. She was annoying, and she was rude, but they'd rescued Godfrey together. And, rather to his surprise, he found there was a part of him that felt sorry for her. It couldn't be easy, living with Aunt Egg.

He sighed. "OK. I found something in

the well. It's a scroll, and it has a list of all the things you have to do to be a knight … and I really really REALLY want to be a Very Noble Knight." He stopped, and waited for Prune to laugh, or to sneer at him – but she didn't.

A huge smile spread across her face, and she said, "A knight? WOWEEEE! Let's both be knights!"

Sam blinked. He hadn't expected this. "Erm …"

"Where's this scroll? Let's have a look!" Prune was jumping up and down with excitement.

Unable to think of anything else to do, Sam pulled the scroll out of his pocket.

Prune looked impressed. "That looks OLD!

Come on – we'll go to the library! We can have a proper look at it in there."

She set off at a run, and Sam followed her, his thoughts whirling. Did Prune really think she could be a knight as well? Were girls knights?

He glanced at the doodlebird on his shoulder. "What do you think, Dandy? Can girls be knights?"

The doodlebird scratched his head. "AWK," he said.

"You don't know? I don't either," Sam told him.

The library was empty.

Prune threw herself into a chair, and gazed expectantly at Sam. "So what does it say? What's the first thing we have to do?"

Very carefully Sam unfolded the scroll.

It felt warm and, much to his amazement, the
words had turned to shining gold.

Greetings to all who wish to be Truly Noble
Knights. Herewith we offer you the tasks
that should be accomplished, in order as hereby
listed, that ye may succeed.

"That's boring. Get to the good bit!" Prune ordered.

Frowning at the golden letters, Sam worked his way through the next sentence.

Task One: Thou shalt find thyself a true companion.

"That's what your father said!"

"Pa? You talked to Pa about it?" Prune stared at Sam.

"Not about the scroll. He doesn't know I've found it," Sam explained. "But I told him I wanted to be a knight, and he said there were rules, but that was the only one he could remember."

"I didn't know Pa knew about knights," Prune said thoughtfully. "I've NEVER heard him talking about that sort of thing."

Sam grinned at her. "I don't think your mother likes him to."

Prune giggled. "'Let's think about the FUTURE, Archie dear!'"

"You're really good at voices," Sam said admiringly.

"I'm good at a lot of things. So, which of us is going to be the knight, and which the True Companion?" Prune stopped as a thought came to her. "Do knights ride horses?"

Sam was doing his best to stay calm, but he had a sick feeling in his stomach. Prune already had a pony … and he didn't. "Erm. Yes."

"Do they ride little brown ponies called Weebles?" Prune's face was anxious.

"I rather think they ride snow-white steeds," Sam said.

"Then that's decided." Prune sat back with

the air of one who had made an important decision. "You can be the knight, and I'll be the True Companion. What do we have to do next?"

A very happy Sam picked up the scroll ... And stared.

"It's gone blank!"

"Blank?" Prune scrambled out of her chair and came to look. "Huh! What rubbish!"

The doodlebird put his head on one side.

"AK AK AKK!"

"What's he saying?" Prune asked.

"He says it's magic. Look! Here's a bit more!"

Gleaming words were gradually appearing, and Prune leant over Sam's shoulder, breathing hard. "*A knight in training is patient ...*" she snorted. "I hate being patient!

Is patient … and doth win but one task a day."

"So we'll have to wait until tomorrow," Sam said.

Prune snorted again. "I suppose we'll have to."

Tingalinga bang bang bang!!!!!

It was the bell for lunch, but Prune didn't move. Instead she went on staring at Sam.

"What's the matter?" he asked.

"I was thinking," she said. "I've never been anyone's true companion before. It might be … OK."

"It will be," Sam said. "Roll on tomorrow!"

Prune dashed for the door. "I'm STARVING! And I can smell chicken stew! HOT chicken stew! Come on!"

And Sam J. Butterbiggins, knight-in-training, followed his True Companion down to lunch.

I never ever EVER thought I'd be a
REAL knight-in-training! But now I am!
And I've already started on my tasks!

I've hidden the scroll in my room. Prune
said that would be best. She says she
doesn't think Aunt Egg would like me to
be a knight and I think she's right. Aunt
Egg and Uncle Archibald were VERY
cheerful this afternoon after their hot
chicken dinner, but they both ate so
much they spent the afternoon asleep
and Prune and I had to play Snakes
and Ladders. She cheated three times.
I don't think True Companions EVER
cheat, but when I told her she threw a
cushion at me.

I can't wait till tomorrow!

Join Sam and Prune
on their second quest!

KNIGHT
IN TRAINING

A HORSE
CALLED DORA

Read on for a sneak peek ...

Hodder
Children's
Books

A division of Hachette Children's Books

A DISASTROUS MORNING

Dear diary.

My ambition is to be a Very Noble
Knight who rides a snow-white
steed (that's the kind of horse
Very Noble Knights ride) and who
does Good Deeds and goes
on quests.

It was nearly time for lunch, and Sam J.
Butterbiggins was sitting up in his tower
bedroom trying to write his diary. There was a
smear of ink on his nose, and his fingers were
an interesting shade of blue – Sam was not a
tidy writer. He sucked the end of his pen, and
looked out of the window.

Outside, the sky was blue and the sun
was shining, and the forest that surrounded
Mothscale Castle on three sides was looking
green and cheerful. Usually it was dark and
gloomy, and Sam suspected that unpleasant
things lurked in the shadows beneath
the trees. Cheered on by
the sunshine, he turned
back to his ink spattered page.

I don't care what
Aunt Egg says.
I'm sure there
are wolves in the
woods. I can hear
them howling at night.
I think the trees move,
too. I'm CERTAIN one
waved to me when I was

looking out of the window yesterday evening.
I waved back, just to see what happened,
and it waved again from a different place!

I wonder if Mother and Father know how
weird Mothscale Castle is?

Sam glanced up at the portrait of his parents
that hung above his bed. They leered happily
into a corner, and Sam shook his head at them.
"It's all very well for you, going away for a
whole year. But what about me? Stuck here
with Aunt Egg and Uncle Archibald, and only
Prune for company—"

"AWK!" The doodlebird perched on the top
of the door gave Sam a reproachful look.

Sam grinned at him. "Sorry, Dandy. And
you, of course. And …" he patted an old and
grubby parchment scroll lying on the table
beside him, "I've got this now!"

The doodlebird nodded several times and flew down to Sam's shoulder. "AWK," he said, and nibbled his ear.

"It's all right," Sam said. "I was just about to write about it." He dipped his pen in the ink-well, and began again.

Guess what ... the most AMAZING thing happened! I found an ancient scroll, and it said,

"Greetings to all who wish to be Truly Noble Knights. Herewith we offer you the tasks that should be accomplished, in order as hereby listed, that ye may succeed."

If I can do all the tasks, then maybe I'll get to be a real knight! But I've only just started.

Task one: Thou shalt find thyself a true companion.

I've actually done that one. My true companion is Prune, my cousin. She's a bit annoying, but not all the time. Also she has a pony called Weebles, so when I get my snow-white steed we'll be able to go on quests together.

At first she wanted to be a knight and I got REALLY worried because I thought I'd have to be the True Companion, but then she changed her mind. PHEW!!!!

I don't know what the other tasks are yet. I'm only allowed to do one a day.

Sam put down his pen. The ancient scroll was beside him, but he'd promised Prune that he wouldn't so much as peep at it until they were alone together. So far, the day had been a disaster. Prune's music teacher had arrived just as they were plotting their escape after breakfast, and Sam had spent most of the morning listening to his cousin trying to play the Mothscale national anthem on the bagpipes. As Prune could only play two notes, the wails and screeches were horrendous. Sam was finally rescued by Uncle Archibald coming out of his office with tufts of cotton wool stuffed in his ears, insisting that the lesson was continued elsewhere. Preferably in Australia, but the garden room would do.

The sound of wheels on the cobbles made Sam look out of the window.

"I expect that's the music teacher leaving," he said to the doodlebird. "Yes ... there he goes. He doesn't look very happy. Still, he's gone, and now Prune and I can get on with the second task!"

GOBLINS

Beware - there are goblins living among us!

Within these pages lies a glimpse into their secret world. But read quickly, and speak softly, in case the goblins spot you...

A riotous, laugh-out-loud funny series for younger readers from the bestselling author of **HUGLESS DOUGLAS**, David Melling.